bigblack35
by Amitz Pamun

Copyright © 2020

All rights reserved. No part of this publication may be reproduced, stored in a retrieval system or transmitted in any form or by any means, electronic, mechanical, photocopying, recording or otherwise, without the prior written permission of the publisher.

ISBN: 9798589104349

Published by: Lucy L. Publishing

lucylleftiepublishing.weebly.com

bigblack35 is owned by Lucy L. Publishing.

Also Available from Amitz Pamun

NOTE: This content is not suitable for children under the age of 18

lucylleftiepublishing.weebly.com

NOTE: This content is not suitable for children under the age of 18

TABLE OF CONTENT

Darrin...5

Jasper...75

Chen...106

Javier...128

Sean...148

Cory...167

Noah...176

DARRIN

In NYC the city that never sleeps, well, until the year 2020, Cory is a man of 35 years, who, after watching "To Catch a Predator," decided on his own terms to get on the other side of the matter. Has he done the right thing, taking the law into his own hands, or has he violated the law by saving possible prey?

Thomas runs towards a school bus. As he gets on, Darrin yells,

"See you later, Tom."

Darrin waves at Thomas. Thomas replies,

"Call me when you get home, Darrin."

"Will do."

Darrin walks home. As he arrives home, he takes his key, unlocks the door and rushes into the empty house. Darrin runs upstairs to his room and shuts the door. Darrin throws his bookbag on his bed and walks to his computer and turns it on. Even though he is aware the house is empty, he looks behind his back to make sure he is home alone. He then enters a password to enter his computer. He then takes off his coat and shoes, walks into the bathroom without closing the door. Urine is heard entering the toilet; a flush and then the sink. Darrin returns to his room and approaches his computer. He goes online, checks again to see if anyone has come home, and then goes to www.unitedchatrooms.com. He then signs in and goes to a chatroom under his favorites (NYCManBoylove). He sits for a while watching the conversation. He sees a message from bigblack35 which reads: Just saying hello. Darrin double clicks on bigblack35 to start a private conversation.

Darrin212: Hey, my name is Darrin. What's yours?

bigblack35: Hello, Darrin. My name is Cory

Darrin212: Hi, Cory. Where do you live?

bigblack35: I'm on 54th St

Darrin212: Oh cool. I live on 65th

bigblack35: Cool. Not far at all.

Darrin212: Yeah. So, what does your screen name mean?

bigblack35: 35 describes my age. Big black describes my dick.

Darrin212: Oh, cool. R u into meeting?

bigblack35: Of course. That's why I'm here. Best chatroom to find cuties to meet. How old are you?

Darrin212: 14. So, what r u into?

bigblack35: I like to get my dick sucked

Darrin212: Cool. Do u suck dick?

bigblack35: yeah.

Darrin212: Cool. Would u be interested in meeting me?

bigblack35: Of course. Where would we meet?

Darrin212: My place is fine.

bigblack35: what about your parents?

Darrin212: It would be when they r not home.

bigblack35: oh.

Darrin212: My dad has a charity dinner to go to. Both my parents will be going. I'll have the house to myself.

bigblack35: r u the only child?

Darrin212: No. I have a sister, but she is away at college.

bigblack35: Cool. So, when can we meet?

Darrin212: Two days from now. Thursday night.

bigblack35: cool.

Darrin212: They should be gone by 630. the charity begins at 7pm.

bigblack35: cool.

Darrin212: U can get here at 7pm

bigblack35: awesome. Where do u live?

Darrin212: 123B 65th St.

bigblack35: cool. I'll be there at 7.

Darrin212: Cool. I'll see u on Thursday night. I cannot wait.

bigblack35: me either. What's your number just in case I need it.

Darrin212: 212 555 2345. It's my cell. You can text if need be. See you then

bigblack35: ok. Thnx.

Darrin closes the chat window and then signs out of unitedchatrooms.com. He then types in freegayporn.net. He surfs the website and begins to rub his private area. He unzips his pants and slides his pants down to his ankles. As he slides off his

10

underwear his cell phone rings. He quickly redresses and answers his phone. He speaks,

"Hey Tom. What's up?"

"You asked me to call you."

"Oh yeah, are you going to the dance?"

"I don't know."

"Why not, man?"

"I don't have anyone to go with."

"You don't have to go with anyone."

"But then I'll look like a looser."

"No, you won't, man. Just go by yourself and if there is someone there you like then just ask her to dance with you."

"It's easier said than done, Darrin."

"It's really not. You just ask."

"It's easy for you to say. All the girls like you. You could go with any girl you want."

"You just have to be likeable, that's all. You can't be so shy."

"I try, but it doesn't work."

"Don't worry about it, man. I'll ask for you."

"No, then I'll definitely look like a punk."

"Well, I don't want to go with out you, and I want to go. So, get yourself together so we can go. Okay?"

"I don't know, Darrin."

"Thomas, come on, man. You're making this more difficult than it has to be."

"I'll think about it."

"You're going, man. Okay?"

"Okay, I guess."

Rita, Darrin's mom opens the door,

"Darrin, did you do your homework, yet?"

"No, ma."

"Hang up the phone and do your homework. I told you about that."

Darrin rolls his eyes, but makes sure his mom doesn't see it. Rita walks out of the room. Darrin finishes his conversation with Thomas,

"Tom, I gotta go."

"Your mom is on your back?"

"You know it. I'll talk to you later."

It is Wednesday evening.

Darrin is in his room on the computer looking up porn. He is barely naked with the door closed and locked.

Rita is in the living room. Every now and again she looks outside the window. There is a car with a black male sitting in the car. She can tell he is hesitating to get out of the car. She is wondering who he is and not sure if she should call the police.

Cory takes a deep breath and then gets out of the car. In his hand is a black case that holds a laptop. He walks towards the door looking around to see if anyone is watching. He finally approaches the door and rings the doorbell. Rita answers the door unsure who this man is and what he wants.

"Yes, sir, may I help you?"

"Hi is this-"

Rita notices the case he is holding. She jumps to conclusions,

"Okay, now look, whatever it is you are selling, I promise you I don't want it."

"Oh, no, ma'am, I'm not trying to sell anything. I need to-"

"Are you a Jehovah Witness? Because what I can't understand is where was ya'll when Jehovah needed a witness. And you should do your research on that occult. Did you know that everyone of your leaders up until the 70's predicted the Rapture and was wrong? You might want to check that out before you barf up that crap at someone's door."

"No, thank you, I am not a Jehovah-"

"Are you a Mormon? "Cause they ain't no better. Listen, I know Jesus, okay. Unlike everyone else in this country I actually take time to read my bible."

"That's good, but this isn't about that."

"Then what is it about?"

"Your son."

Rita gets concerned. Her defense is up higher than the sky.

"What do you mean and who the hell are you?

"This is 123B 65th St, correct?

16

"Well, yes. Sir, who are you? What is going on?

Cory takes the laptop out of the case. He opens it and already has the unitedchatroom dialog he had with Darrin on the screen.

"Would you mind stepping out here? You should read this."

Rita reluctantly closes the door and reads the screen,

"What is this?"

"Darrin212 is your son."

"If you don't take that out of my face, I will call the police."

"Before you do anything you regret, please just let me explain."

"Get out of here!"

"You and your husband are going to a charity dinner on Thursday, correct? And Darrin's cell phone number is 212 555-2345, correct?"

With much shock and a little bit of fear Rita takes a moment before she answers,

"How did you know that?"

Cory with caution continues,

"Darrin contacted me in a chatroom called NJ Man/Boy Love. It's a chatroom where men can meet boys for sex. I'm supposed to be meeting him here on Thursday night while you and your husband go to that dinner. Darrin doesn't know this, but I have no intentions on being here. I came here a day early so I can tell you what's going on. Now, before you yell at him, you might want to know that statistics prove that any child interested in having sex with an adult, has been, or is being molested. I came here so that you can be aware of this. Punishing him is not the answer. He needs help. Professional help."

Cory takes a business card out of his pocket,

"This woman can help. She is a great therapist. Your son is not a bad person he has just been broken. I suggest you don't mention anything to your husband yet?"

Rita responds quickly with anger,

"Why not?"

"Because statistically, molestation is mostly incest. Being that Darrin is attracted to older men it means that it was an older man who molested him. Now I am not

19

saying his father molested him, but I wouldn't count it out. The best thing you can do is find a way to talk to Darrin, where he does not feel ashamed, afraid, or attacked, in order for you to figure out who his first sexual experience was."

"You come here with your fancy old computer and show me some filth and I am supposed to believe my son was molested by his father. Who the hell do you think you are?"

"I did not say that. You have to understand my concern. Not just for your son, but for the other boys."

"What other boys?"

"Your son is looking for sex online which means there is a high percent chance that he is not being molested any more. He still enjoys the sex, but can't get it from the man who originally molested him."

Rita not convinced replies,

"If he was molested?"

"Listen, whoever molested him did it when Darrin was younger. Darrin got too old for him so now he, the child molester, has or is seeking another boy. That's just how it works. I came over here hoping you will see the urgency to get Darrin help."

"What time were you supposed to be here on Thursday?"

"He told me 7pm because you and your husband would be leaving by 6:30pm because the dinner begins at 7PM. I also know about your daughter away at college."

"Why would he tell you that?"

"That was basically assurance that I and he would be alone the entire time. He needs help. I can promise you I am not the first person he has contacted. And sadly, enough he probably has had already had some guests over. Do you leave him alone often?"

Rita with much shock and guilt replies,

"Not often, but often enough."

"It's not your fault. You didn't know."

"But I should have. I should have never trusted a child could be home alone. I should have gotten a babysitter."

"I suggest you do that for Thursday. This way he can cancel our night together and I won't have to explain who I am and what I do.

"What do you do?"

"I stop boys like your son from having sex with men."

Rita looks up to the sky in disbelief and gives a shocking deep breathe,

"Well, I'll see if I can get a babysitter."

Cory continues,

"I am sorry if I offended you, but I promise you everything I said is the truth and you really should seek help for Darrin. And please, do not make him feel guilty. I promise you he already has more than enough guilt and shame on his shoulders."

"Well, I am going to check, and if everything you are saying is not true, I will go to the authorities and have you arrested." Cory takes out another business card.

"This is all my information. If I am wrong you can give them this. Again, I apologize for catching you off guard, but it needed to be done. I will leave you alone now."

Cory puts the note book back in its case and walks back to his car. He gets in and drives away. Rita watches him as he drives away. She has fear of telling her husband, Michael. She thinks about what Cory said about incest. She looks at the business cards. As she stands in fear, her husband arrives. He gets out of the car and notices Rita standing in a daze. Michael speaks,

"Is everything okay?"

"Yeah. Why?"

"You're standing outside in the daze holding business cards. That's not necessarily normal."

"Oh. Right. No need to be alarmed all is well."

"Can we go inside?"

"Sure."

Rita and Michael walk into the house. As Michael goes to his room, Rita follows. He puts his brief case down and then starts to undress. Rita just stares not sure what to say. Michael notices and asks,

"Is everything okay?"

"Um. Do you mind if we talk?"

"Sure, what's wrong?"

"Nothing is wrong. I was thinking that maybe we should get a babysitter for Darrin."

"Why?"

"Because he's a teenager now and you know, I don't think he should be home alone tomorrow, that's all."

"He's been alone for the past year ever since Heather left for college. Why the sudden care?"

"Well, you know: house parties or inviting guests over. Us not being home may cause him to have people over."

"He's never done that in the past."

"We don't know that. They could have left before we got back."

Michael sees the concern in Rita's eyes, not sure what to think or say, and for lack of arguing, agrees with her.

"Okay...if you think that's what is best...then. Who are you going to get at such late notice?"

"Well, our neighbor has a daughter in community college. Kathleen is always bragging about how responsible her daughter is, so I thought I'd ask her."

"Um...okay. Uh...should we pay her?"

"Of course, hun."

"How much?"

"Don't worry about the fee. I'll take care of it."

Michael with concern, looks into Rita's eyes,

"Rita."

"Yes, Michael."

"Is everything okay?"

"Sure, Michael. Everything is…just fine. What did you want for dinner?"

"Anything is fine."

Rita walks away not sure how to continue her life. Not sure if Cory was the real deal or maybe she dreamed it, she is unsure of herself, her husband, and her son.

Thursday evening arrives and Michael and Rita are preparing to go to their fundraiser. Thankfully, Samantha, Kathleen's responsible daughter was available to babysit.

Darrin walks into the living room, unaware of the new arrangements, and notices Samantha in the living room watching television.

"Samantha? What are you doing here?"

"Hi Darrin. Your parents hired me to baby sit you tonight."

"What? Really?"

"Yes. Is that a problem?"

"No, of course not. I just…it's nothing."

Darrin with anxious shock walks upstairs to his parents' bedroom.

Rita is in a house coat sitting in front of a mirror. She has rollers in her hair and she is applying makeup. Darrin enters and notices her,

    "Mom, why is Samantha here?"

    "She's going to be babysitting."

    "But, I'm not a baby."

    "Then, consider her a chaperone."

    "Why do I need a chaperone? I've been home alone many times."

Rita stops to think about that statement and realizes each time Darrin was alone, he may have not been alone. She pauses before she continues,

    "It's just a decision I have made. If you're hungry, there's food on the stove."

"I don't understand why out of nowhere you decided I needed to be chaperoned."

"We will talk about this later, Darrin. Go do your homework."

Rita continues with her make-up. Darrin sighs heavily and then walks out of the room. Rita watches him as he exits the room. She has such sorrow on her face.

Darrin is sitting on his bed apparently upset. He receives a text. Darrin gets his phone to reads the text.

CORY: Hey, this is Cory. R we still on 4 tonight?

DARRIN: No. my mom decided to get a chaperone. I

> *won't be home alone. I'll contact you at another time.*
>
> *CORY: Oh darn. No problem, man. We'll meet another time.*

Darrin upset responds,

> "Damn."

Michael and Rita are at the fundraiser. Music, dancing, eating, and fun is in the air. Rita is standing with two women. She is spaced out as they converse.

> "Ooh, Dana, do you see Mrs. Matthews? She is totally eating everything in sight. She is being so rapacious."
>
> "I know, Sarah. She needs to go on Weight Watchers or Jenny Craig."

"I know what you mean. And look at Mr. Phillips over there; just flirting with everything in heels."

"I know. I'm surprise his wife has staid with him all this time. Ooh, Sarah, look over there. Ms. Opal Richardson. She is such an adulteress."

"I heard she's having an affair with Mr. Phillips."

"I'm not surprised. Those two deserve each other."

Sarah notices Rita is zoned out and not mentally in the room,

"Are you okay, Rita?"

Rita responds,

"What?"

"Girl, what is wrong with you?"

"What do you mean?"

Dana responds,

"My goodness, Rita, you are completely spaced out."

Sarah continues,

"What's on your mind?"

"Nothing."

Sarah with excitement responds,

"Ooh, girl you got some new gossip?"

Dana follows up,

"Girl, spill it."

"No, it's nothing like that. I just. It's nothing."

Dana responds,

"It's nothing, usually means, it's something."

Sarah continues,

"Girl, what is it?"

Rita begins to speak, but stops.

"I'm going to go outside and get some fresh air."

Sarah responds,

"Girl, the smokers are outside. There is no fresh air out there."

Rita walks out of the room and steps outside. Sarah speaks to Dana,

"Girl, I'll be right back."

Sarah follows Rita outside. Dana walks towards another set of ladies and converses with them.

As Sarah approaches Rita, she notices the smokers,

"See, girl, what did I tell you? There is nothing, but nicotine in the air. There is no fresh air out here."

Rita asks,

"Do you feel bad leaving your children home alone?"

"No. Why?"

"I thought I wanted to go back to work once my children were in school. I'm not so sure any more. I mean there should be someone home when they get home."

"Your children are grown; they don't need anyone home."

"Darrin is not grown, and neither is Heather."

"What brought this on, Rita?"

Rita looks at Sarah for a moment. She then nods her head no,

"I don't know if I can talk about it right now."

Sarah continues,

"Rita, you can trust me. It's not like I gossip."

"When it's time for me to talk to you, will you promise to support me?"

"Yes, girl. Of course. What is wrong?"

"I…I can't tell you right now, but one day…I believe I will."

Friday, the next day, Rita comes home from work. She looks at the stairs knowing Darrin is in his room. She knows she needs to speak to him, but is afraid. She sighs at the stairs as if they are Mount Everest. She walks up the stairs slowly. As she gets closer her heart pounds like the drums of a fast-paced song. She gets to Darrin's door and knocks. Darrin knowing what time she comes home has already put away his computer. He opens the door,

    "Hey, ma."

    "Hi, son. Darrin, I need to talk to you."

Not liking the tone in her voice or her body language, Darrin fearfully asks,

    "About what?"

Rita sits on Darrin's bed. She immediately thinks of all the men who might have been in the bed with Darrin.

"Please, sit."

"Mom, what is wrong?"

"I want to talk about why I hired Samantha. Firstly, I want you to know that I am not angry with you. I want you to know that I love you and that you can trust me."

"Mom, why are you talking like this? What is wrong?"

Rita takes a deep breathe,

"Remember now, I am not upset with you, okay?"

"Ma!"

"Can you tell me who bigblack35 is?"

Darrin with much surprise and fear pauses not sure what to say,

"Who?"

"Darrin. You know who."

Like a broken faucet his tears begin to flow down his face,

"I don't know."

"I told you; you can trust me. I'm not upset, Darrin. I just need you to talk to me. Who is he?"

"I don't know."

"Has he been here?"

"No."

"Was that your first time contacting a man?"

"Mom…I don't know what you are talking about?"

"Why are you afraid to talk to me? I am not upset. I won't punish you, I just need you to trust me. Was that your first time?"

Like a river, a flushing mighty river, Darrin has tears flowing heavily. He breathes heavily,

"No."

Rita puts her head down. She then lifts her head and sighs heavily. Her tears are matching her son's.

"Has anyone ever come here when you were alone? When your father and I were gone?"

Darrin takes a moment then responds,

"Does dad know?"

"No."

Darrin takes a breath of relief. Rita continues,

"Darrin. Has anyone ever come to this house?"

Darrin continues to cry,

"I'm sorry, mom."

Disappointed, Rita tries her best not to show any anger emotions as not to put fear into Darrin.

"How many?"

Darrin takes a pause to think.

"I've never counted."

Rita pauses for a moment,

"Has it been that many?"

"No. not really."

"Can you take a guess?"

Darrin looks up to count in his head,

"I don't know. Maybe three or four."

Rita in a frustrated and angry voice responds,

"Four men!?

She catches herself,

"I'm sorry. I didn't mean to…"

Rita stops to think for a while.

"When did this begin?"

Darrin's eyes look around for a bit before answering.

"I was twelve."

Rita stops to think.

"Why would you do this?"

"I don't know. I just did."

"Do you enjoy it?"

Darrin frustrated with the question,

"Ma!"

Rita takes a small break.

"So, at twelve…was that your first sexual experience?"

"Ma, please."

"Was that your first time?"

Darrin looks down for a moment and then looks around,

"How did you find out about this?"

"Cory came over and told me. He suggested I get a chaperone so he wouldn't have to cancel your date."

"What is he, the police?"

"I don't know. But he told me something that worries me."

"What?"

"He said the only child who would seek sex is one who has been molested. Is that true?"

Darrin doesn't speak out of shame.

"I don't know."

"Darrin, I love you. There is nothing you can say that will make me ashamed of you. Please, Darrin, answer the question. Were you molested?"

Darrin pauses with shame. While tears fall down his face like a waterfall he responds,

"Yeah."

Rita takes a deep breathe,

"Thank you, for trusting me. Can we take the next step?"

"What next step?"

"How old were you when it first happened?"

Darrin closes his eyes and pauses before answering.

"Seven."

Rita flashbacks, trying to figure out when it could have happened and who it could have been. Trying to think back seven years ago is not easy when you have just been told your child was abused. With fear and anxiousness, she takes him by his hands. Darrin looks at her. She looks him in his eyes; he looks back.

"Who was it?"

Darrin looks away and moves his hands. He then wipes his tears.

"I don't think I can do that yet."

Rita takes a deep breathe.

"Was it your father?"

"No!"

"Then why is it so difficult? Tell me, please.

No response from Darrin.

"Darrin, please. Who was it?"

Darrin takes a deep breath and looks up,

"Uncle Scott"

Rita lets go a deep sigh,

"Oh, my gosh."

Rita stands and then paces the room. She is breathing heavily as if she is going into labor. She is trying to do more than pace and breath, but she is lost for words. She finally grabs Darrin and she embraces him with a hug. A hug of empathy and apology. Both, Darrin and Rita cry into each other's arms.

Friday, Saturday, and Sunday have passed. Rita has yet to get the courage to tell Michael about Darrin and Cory. She told

Darrin to keep quiet until she figures it out. It is Monday and Rita knows she must do something. After work she takes a ride to her brother's house, Scott. With much shock and fear she rings the doorbell. Scott answers the door,

"Hey, Rita. What are you doing here?"

"Can't a sister visit her brother?"

"Of course. I just wish you would have called. I'm not really prepared for visitors."

"It's okay. I just need to speak with you about something important?"

"Is everything okay?"

"May I come in?"

"Of course."

Rita and Scott walk into the living room. She notices a boy about the age of seven. With caution she asks,

"And who is this?"

Scott replies,

"Tyrone, he's the neighbor's son. I'm babysitting. His parents don't come home until after 5pm. They don't like him home alone so he comes here after school and his mom picks him up after work.

Rita afraid for the boy responds,

"Oh."

"Well, what did you want to talk about?"

"I don't think now is the time. You have company."

"Oh, please. We can talk. Did you want to go upstairs?"

"No. How often does he come over here?"

"Mondays through Fridays. Basically, whenever his parents are at work."

"Oh, okay."

Rita looks at Tyrone,

"And how are you doing, Tyrone? Are you okay?"

Tyrone answers

"Yes, ma'am."

Scott speaks to Tyrone,

"Tyrone, this is my sister, Rita."

"Hi, Ms. Rita."

"Hi, Tyrone, it was nice to meet you."

Rita hugs Scott.

"It was nice to see you again. I will come by later. Probably tomorrow."

"Sure, just call first, okay?"

"Sure. Not a problem."

Scot and Rita walk towards the door.

"Oh, I can let myself out."

"You sure."

"Yeah."

Rita leaves the house. She is troubled, not sure of what to do with the situation at hand. She gets into her car,

"God, please, don't let it be...don't let it be so, please.

She drives the roads frantically. There must be an angel watching over her, because her driving should get her a ticket, but thankfully for her, no police are around. When she sees a pay phone, she parks the car at a diner. She puts on gloves and tries to conceal herself. She gets out of the car and walks to the pay phone. She picks up the phone and dials 911. The operator picks up.

"911, what's your emergency?"

Rita disguises her voice,

"I think a boy is being molested."

"Who's speaking please?"

"You can find the boy at 321X 76th St in New York City—

"Who's speaking please?"

"The boy is usually there between the hours of three and 5PM, Monday through Fridays. You should get there around 4PM. I think the man who watches him is molesting him. His name is—"

Rita starts crying.

"Who's speaking please? Ma'am, are you there?"

"The man's name is Scott".

"Ma'am, what is Scott's last name…Ma'am…ma'am, are you there? What is his last name?"

Rita hangs up the phone. She cries in the booth.

About three hours later Robert and Patricia, Tyrone's parents are running into a hospital.

53

They stop at the front desk. There is a police officer standing there. The couple approaches the front desk. Patricia speaks first,

"Where is my baby?"

The nurse at the front desk responds,

"Excuse me?"

Robert responds,

"Tyrone! Tyrone Stephens, where is he?"

The police officer standing there recognizes the name and responds,

"Are you Tyrone Stephen's parents?"

Robert anxiously responds,

"Yes. Where is he?"

54

"Hi, my name is Officer Jackson. Follow me."

Patricia asks,

"What happened?"

"There was an anonymous 911 call stating that your son was being molested by the guy who was babysitting him."

Robert with the reaction most fathers would have responds,

"I'm going to kill him. Where is Scott?"

The police officer answers,

"Scott is at the station being questioned. Your son was being tested to see if he had any signs of sexual abuse."

As they walk, they approach Detective Perez and Detective Lee.

The police officer speaks,

"Detectives, these are Tyrone's parents. "

"Hello, I'm Detective Perez and this is Detective Lee. We're from special victims' unit. We're just waiting for the doctor."

"I'm Robert Stephens and this is my wife Patricia."

Detective Lee responds,

"I'm really sorry we had to meet under these circumstances. We just have to wait to see if any of this is true. The police station received an anonymous call. The woman wouldn't give her name. She just gave Scott's name and address, as well as the fact that there would be a boy there whom she believed to be abused."

"Well, how long is it going to take?"

Detective Perez answers,

"It shouldn't be long."

The doctor enters the hallway. Detective Perez continues,

"Oh good. Doctor Robinson this is Tyrone's parents, Robert and Patricia."

Patricia asks,

"Is everything okay?"

Doctor Robinson answers,

"Tyrone is doing okay. He's in the children's room with a child's psychologist."

"Why?"

"There were signs of abuse."

"I'm going to kill that bastard."

The doctor continues,

"I hate to tell you this, but there were fluids in and around his rectal area.

Patricia cries out,

"Oh my gosh. Why?"

Robert continues,

"I'm killing him."

The doctor continues,

"There was also amylase found on his penis."

Robert asks,

"What the hell is that!"

"Enzymes found in saliva."

"Ah, shit! I'm killing him."

Detective Perez speaks,

"Mr. Stephens, with all due respects you must calm down and let us do our job."

Detective Lee speaks to Doctor Robinson.

"Has Tyrone said anything to Dr. Evans, yet?"

"Not yet. But she is getting close."

Patricia with concern responds,

"I want to see him."

Doctor Robinson responds,

Now, wouldn't be a good time. The psychologist, Dr. Evans, needs this time with him. The only way Scott is going to prison is with a witness.

Robert just noticing what the doctor said speaks with rage,

"What the fuck do you mean? That bitch's cum was in my son's ass."

59

Patricia responds,

"Damn, Robert, you didn't have to say it like that."

Detective Lee responds,

"Scott hasn't been completely cooperative. We don't have his DNA so we cannot prove at this moment whose liquids they are."

Robert responds,

"This is straight up shit!"

Patricia massages Robert,

"Babe, please, calm down."

Detective Perez responds,

"I know how angry you are, but I am going to do every thing I can to make sure he goes to prison."

Doctor Robinson speaks,

"Please allow me to suggest Dr. Evans. Your son is going to need therapy and she is highly recommended."

Patricia responds,

"Thank you, Doctor Robinson."

It has now been a week since Scott has been arrested. Cory is typing at his computer. He is in the process of setting up another meeting on unitedchatrooms.com. The television is on. As he types the news anchor speaks,

"In breaking news, a couple needs your help. They, for security purposes, will remain nameless, but they need you to help their son. If you or anyone you know has been molested by Scott Anderson, the man in the photo on your screen, please get in contact with the police. For more information we now take it to the court house, with Laura Singer."

"Thank you, Kendra. Earlier today, here at the court house the district attorney, Opal Right, made a statement."

"My name is Opal Right, and I am the District attorney on this case. We really need your help. If you know of anyone or if you yourself have been molested by Scott Anderson, we ask that you step forward so that we can put this man in prison where he cannot harm any more children. Please call our hotline 123-555-3456 or stop by your local police station. We are asking you to help this family and to help this community get rid of a child predator. Thank you for your time."

About a day after the breaking news, Michael, Rita, and Darrin walk into the police station and approach the front desk. Darrin approaches the officer at the front desk. He hesitates to speak. Michael responds,

"Go ahead, Darrin."

Darrin hesitates again and then looks at his mom, afraid to turn her mom's brother in, Rita assures him,

"It's okay."

The officer speaks,

"May I help you?"

Darrin speaks,

"Yeah. I…uh. I came here in regards of my Uncle Scott. Scott Anderson."

The officer responds,

"Oh. He's your uncle. I guess you came here to defend him; to tell us he's innocent."

Darrin reluctantly responds,

"I came here to tell you that I am…I was one of his victims."

Oh, my goodness. It was brave of you to come in here and do this. Just wait over there. I will have an officer take you in a room so they can question you."

Michael, Rita, and Darrin sit in the waiting area. As they wait patiently a young gentleman walks in and looks around. Officer Williams notice he looks lost,

"May I help you, sir?"

The young man approaches her,

"Yes. My name is Brian Gregor. I'm here about the...uh...Scott Anderson thing."

Michael, Rita, and Darrin look at him in shock waiting to see what he has to say.

The officer responds,

"What is it, sir?"

"It might be too late. It was about fourteen years ago. He uh, you know, molested me."

Rita grabs Michael and sobs. Michael holds her in comfort.

After a month of victims coming forth, Scott decided to come forth with the truth. Scott plead guilty to twelve counts of endangerment of a child. Four of his victims were still minors and the other eight were adults who came forth. There were more adults, but they came forth too late. Scott received three years per eligible count making it thirty-six years behind bars. He will be eligible for early dismissal on good behavior. He also has to get counseling as well as register as a sex offender once he is released. About three months after the case, Rita takes the trip to prison to visit her brother.

Rita is sitting in the meeting room waiting for Scott to arrive. When Scott enters the room and notices Rita, he approaches her with his head down. He is crying and is flooded with guilt and shame. He reluctantly sits down. His head is down and he cannot seem to look at Rita. Rita responds,

"Scott, come on. Look at me."

"I can't."

"You don't have to be ashamed. You know, I forgive you, right? So does Darrin and Michael too."

"Why are you here?"

"I wanted to visit you."

"Why?"

"You're still family. I love you. I hate what you did, but I still love you."

"Why aren't you angry with me?"

"I am, but I still forgive you."

"Why? I ruined your son."

"He's not ruined. He's broken, but God can fix him. He can even fix you."

"I want you to be angry with me."

"Why?"

"It makes me feel horrible that you are not mad at me."

"Being angry is not going to change the past."

She quickly changes the subject.

"The cassette tapes I brought you will help you."

"What is it?"

"It's called Spiritual Warfare. It will help you fight the demons. The ones that make you attracted to boys."

"Why are you being so nice to me?"

"Because I love you."

A short pause. Rita continues,

"May I ask you a question?"

"What?"

"I heard…someone once told me that…someone told me basically the only reason why a person would do what you did is because it was already done to them. Is that true?"

Scott sighs heavily?

"Yeah."

"How come you never told me?"

"I was afraid. Then I became too ashamed to tell."

"Why would you be ashamed?"

"Because I started to enjoy it."

Rita pauses before she asks,

"Who was it?"

Scott takes a pause and then sighs,

"Wilson."

"You mean Coach Wilson?"

"Yeah."

"What happened?"

Scott sighs, looks up while the tears fall down,

"One day after practice he had asked me, Billy Parks, and Mathew Rice to stay behind. He said he wanted to share some special plays to his best players. We felt special. Once all the other boys were gone…it happened…it took me some time to realize that we weren't his best players…we were just the only players that walked home alone. He knew our parents weren't coming to pick us up. We talked about it all the time and didn't know what to do. By the time we were thirteen he had picked a new set of boys. The three of us continued on our own. By the time college started I was hooked. I had some hook ups in college, but as I got older, I just desired boys. I hated myself. I felt trapped. Trapped between guilt, shame, and temptation. I wanted it, but I knew I shouldn't…every time I got away with it…it just made me want it more."

He pauses then he continues,

    "They told me an anonymous caller turned me in."

There is a pause. Rita's eyes sway from side to side nervously. Scott continues,

"I know it was you."

Another silence between the two of them. Scott continues,

"Thank you. I needed someone to stop me. Because I couldn't. Thank you. Thank you, for being brave and speaking up. I wanted to, but I couldn't seem to do it."

Scott begins to cry. The tears fill his eyes and roll down his cheeks. He continues,

"I need you to let Darrin know how sorry I am for what I did to him. It was inexcusable."

Rita and Scott are crying. Rita responds,

"He knows already. I told you, he forgives you. He chose to forgive you. Michael too. We love you, Scott. We're no different from God. We hate everything you did, but what you did is not who you are. And we love you. Okay?"

Scott cries and responds,

"Thank you. Thank you for loving me."

There is a pause as they both wipe their tears off their faces. Scott continues,

"I heard a saying once that said: You never know the love someone has for you until it has been tested. I guess this is my love test."

JASPER

Cory walks into a diner with his black case. As he enters the diner, the greeter immediately slaps on a smile and speaks,

"Hi, sir. Is it just one?"

Cory responds,

"I am looking for a waitress who works here. I'm not sure of her name, but I believe she has a son named, Jasper."

The greeter responds,

"Oh, that's Melanie's son. Is everything okay?"

"Yeah. I need to speak with her though."

"Hold on."

The greeter walks to the kitchen. When she returns, Melanie is with her. The greeter speaks to Cory,

"Here she is. I have to get back to work now."

The greeter proceeds to help the other customers. Melanie speaks to Cory,

"May I help you? Is everything okay with my son?"

"I need to speak with you. Possibly in private."

"Why? What's going on?"

"I can't explain right now."

"Well, I'm working. Is it urgent?"

"It is. And it cannot wait. Would you be able to ask your boss for a quick break? Just tell him or her that it's an urgent

76

family matter. I promise I won't keep you long."

"Wait here."

Melanie walks over to her boss and tells her what's going on. There is some conversation before her boss allows her to see Cory. Melanie thanks her boss and then approaches Cory. Melanie returns,

"This better be important. What is it?"

"Can you come outside with me please? It's private."

"What is going on?"

"Please, just come outside."

Melanie agrees. Cory walks outside, Melanie follows him. Cory walks to his car. Melanie responds,

"What is going on here? And where is my son? Is he with you? Do I have to call the police?"

"Not now. They won't do you any help, but soon you will."

Melanie gets really concerned,

"What is going on?"

"I need you to do me a favor."

"I don't even know you."

"My name is Cory. Do you always work the night shift?"

"Only on weekdays. I need the money. What's it to you anyway?"

"Jasper told me about you. How you're usually not home because you're working."

"Are you from child services? You're not taking my son away from me."

"No. Read this."

Cory takes out the laptop of the case. He opens it and shows Melanie the conversation between him and Jasper. Melanie looks at the laptop screen. She soon drops open her mouth in shock.

"What is that filth? Are you some kind of perv?"

"No. Bigblack35 is me and Jay12apt3a is Jasper.

"You disgusting pig. I'm calling the police."

Melanie goes to leave, but Corey grabs her arm,

"Listen, please, I am trying to help you."

"How is this helping me?"

"Listen to me. You need to get a chaperone or a babysitter for Jasper. I am supposed to be meeting him tomorrow night for sex."

"You're a child rapist?"

"No. That's just the thing I'm trying to tell you. Jasper contacted me through this chatroom."

"How do I know this is Jasper?"

"Look at the user name."

"That means nothing. Many boys have a nickname of Jay."

"Where do you live?"

"I'm not telling you that."

"I already know, Jasper told me. Look at the username. Where do you live?"

She looks at the name again and then with shock grasps for air.

"Oh my gosh."

Cory continues,

"Jay12apt3a. He told me you live at 12 54th St, apartment 3A. If you don't get a chaperone there will be no reason for him to cancel our date. And if I cancel it might look suspicious. You need to get a chaperone for tomorrow night. Then you need to find some time in your busy schedule to sit down and talk to him. He's not a bad child, okay? He's just hurt. He needs help."

"I always felt guilty leaving him home alone, but I needed to work."

"Don't go blaming yourself. It's not your fault."

"Why is he doing this? Why is he attracted to men, like this? He's too young to be doing this."

"That's the next thing I need to talk to you about."

"What?"

Cory takes out a business card,

"She is a great psychologist."

"I don't have money for a doctor."

"Don't worry about that, I'll ask her to bill me."

"Why the hell would you do that?"

"Jasper needs help. Listen, you have to understand that there is a high chance the reason Jasper is attracted to men is because he was molested."

"NO. No…not my baby. He would have told me."

"I know you don't want to hear that, but it's true. You have to take some time to yourself and take this all in. Then you need to sit down and talk with him. He needs to know that he can trust you. You cannot be angry, upset, or even punish him. You need to assure him that you love him and that there is no reason to be afraid or ashamed. That is the only way you're going to get any truth out of him."

Melanie is crying,

"Is this a game? Are you playing a cruel trick on me? Because if you are; you are just disgusting."

"I would not do this for fun. I am not only doing this for Jasper, but for the other boys?"

"What other boys?"

"Any child molester who hasn't been caught keeps going until he stops himself or gets caught. Now there is a chance that Jasper's molester got helped, but there is no way of us knowing. You have to figure out who did this to him and then go to the police."

"I just can't understand this."

"I know. This is not something anyone wants to hear, but the best thing you can do right now is take the steps to fix this."

"Why is this happening?"

Cory embraces Melanie as she cries. He rubs her back in comfort. Soon he releases her,

"Are you going to be able to get back to work?"

"I need to go home."

"Not now. You won't be of any help yet. You're still in shock."

Melanie concerned asks,

"Can I ask you a question?"

"Sure."

"You said he contacted you, right?"

"Yes."

"Do you think you were the first?"

Cory takes a moment to find the words.

"There is always the chance that I was his first, but there's more of a chance I am not the first."

Melanie sobs. Cory embraces her again,

"I know it's difficult, but you have to pull yourself together. Not only for Jasper, but you have to go back to work."

"It's a slow night. I'm going to ask her if I can leave early. I can't work under these circumstances."

"Just make sure when you get home you don't mention anything. Just get someone to watch him and talk to him after tomorrow night. And one other thing."

"What?"

"Jasper never mentioned his father. Is he in the picture?"

"Not really. He visits his dad about twice a month. Why?"

"I wouldn't mention anything to his father just yet."

"Why not?"

"Until Jasper tells you who molested him, you want to make every male in his life a suspect."

"He would never."

"There is at least one person who thinks that about every child molester. Talk to your son, okay. And make sure you call Dr. Zachman. Did you want me to walk you back to the diner?"

"Sure."

Cory escorts her back in to the diner.

The next day Melanie decides not to go to work. She is sitting on the couch of her living room. She is contemplating what to tell her son. The front door is heard being unlocked and then opened. Jasper then enters the room,

    "Hey, ma."

Melanie responds in somber,

    "Hey. Do you mind if I talk to you? It's important."

    "What's wrong?"

    "Can you sit please?"

Jasper sits,

    "Mom, you're scaring me. What's going on?"

Melanie sighs heavily and then continues,

"A man came to me at work last night and I must say I am somewhat speechless right now of what to tell you. I am hoping that this strange man is wrong, but I have a feeling he is not."

"What man?"

"Bigblack35"

Jasper responds in a way that proves he knows who this man is. He hesitates to speak,

"Who...who is that?"

"You tell me, Jasper."

"I'm not sure I know who that is."

"Has he been here?"

"No."

Melanie pauses and then responds,

"Jasper, he's not coming to meet with you. He showed me the things the two of you were talking about on unitedchatrooms. Why would you give him that information? Don't you know there are crazy people out there? He could have been a murderer. What made you do that?"

"I don't know. I was curious."

"Are you gay?"

"I…I…I don' know."

"Was this your first time?"

"What do you mean?"

"Has there been a strange man in this house with you?"

Jasper hangs his head and then shrugs his shoulder. Melanie responds,

"What do you mean you don't know? Either you did or you didn't."

Jasper lifts his head his eyes are filled with tears of fear,

"I was curious. I just wanted to know what…you know…I didn't mean any harm."

"So, this is true?"

"I'm sorry, mom."

"Are you gay, Jasper?"

"I don't know. I just like to…I don't want to talk about it."

"Jasper, I cannot just leave this alone. Those men are abusing you."

"No, I wanted it."

"Jasper, they are not supposed to do those things to you. How many have there been?"

"It was only three."

"Jasper, that's still too many. I cannot believe this."

"Am I in trouble?

"No. But, I need to know how old you were when you first started doing this."

"I don't know. About two years ago."

"What caused you to do this? Were you molested?"

Jasper hesitates to answer,

"I'm sorry mom. I didn't mean to hurt you."

"I'm not hurt. You haven't answered my question. Were you molested?"

"Would you mind if I went to bed? I'm pretty tired."

"No. We're going to talk about this. Now answer me. Have you been molested?"

Jasper pauses. He slowly hangs his head.

"I really didn't want it to happen. I'm sorry mom."

"Why are you apologizing? This isn't your fault."

"You don't understand. It's more than you think."

"What do you mean?"

"I never thought I would have to tell you this."

"WHAT?!"

"I'm sorry."

"Don't be sorry, just talk to me. What happened?"

"Do you remember Brody?"

"Of course, I do. What does he have to do with any of this? Jasper just looks at Melanie."

"Oh, no. You mean Brody...I don't believe this."

"I'm sorry this happened."

"This is not your fault. Are you sure Brody did this?"

"That's just the thing mom. That's what I never wanted to tell you. I didn't realize it until I got older, but..."

"But, what?"

"The first time you left me with Brody alone he molested me. I was scared,

94

but I trusted him. I was ten at the time. He made me feel like it was okay so I never said anything. When he broke up with you, I was confused. I thought it was something I did wrong."

"It was nothing either of us did. He left me for a younger and prettier girl."

Melanie stops to think,

"Come to think of it that girl he left me for has a young son. He didn't leave me. He left you for a younger boy."

Realizing what Brody did, she responds with grief,

"That is disgusting. This is all my fault. I should have been more attentive to you. I should have noticed something. I'm sorry, Jasper."

"It's okay, mom. I'm sorry I didn't tell you earlier."

Melanie stands and hugs Jasper,

"I am sorry I neglected you. I am really sorry this had to happen to you. I am going to fix this."

Jasper lets go of his mother in fear.

"What are you going to do?"

"Don't worry about that. Just know that I am going to make this up to you. I am really sorry that I allowed such a horrible person in your life; our life. I am really going to make this right."

Before going to work, the next day, Melanie stops by a hair salon. She goes inside and waits by the register. A woman at the desk welcomes her,

"Hi, welcome to La Fric Salon. Do you have an appointment?"

Melanie responds,

"I need to speak with Victoria."

"She's on break. Did she say she would do your hair?"

"It's not about that. It's a personal matter. It's urgent."

"Oh, okay. What's your name?"

"Would you please go get her. It's really urgent."

The woman reluctantly goes into the back room and summons Victoria. About two to three minutes later the two women return.

As Vitoria notices Melanie she rolls her eyes,

"Melanie, what do you want?"

"I need to speak with you."

"I'm at work. Besides, I have nothing to say to you. Get over it, okay. He left you and doesn't want you. Stop being such a baby and let him go."

"This is a serious matter. It's about your son."

"Melanie, if you touch my son, I will call the police on you."

"You will need the police, but not for me."

"What are you going on about?"

"Can we please step outside."

"Are you trying to fight me? I do not fight over a man. If he's that special to you, you can have him."

"It's not that at all. I don't want to discuss this in public. Please, step outside." Victoria reluctantly walks outside with Melanie. She responds,

"You know, Melanie, you look really sad and desperate coming here at my job. Brody left you. Why can't you just accept that?"

"Victoria, listen. I met Brody when my son was ten years old. He was at a Christmas party and I ran into him. I'm just realizing now he must have been watching me with my son because… anyway, I just found out that he…well…okay…he broke up with me and he wouldn't explain why. It was weird. He…um…I…uh…"

"What the hell are you trying to tell me?"

"I could be wrong, but I think your son is in danger."

"What? Why?"

"My son just confessed to me that Brody molested him. I think Brody broke up with me not for you, but for your son."

"Are you crazy?"

"No. My son is fifteen now. I honestly thought Brody was going to propose to me. We spent nearly five great years together and then he just broke it off. And it now all makes sense. He left me for you, but he really didn't leave me; he left my son for yours. Brody likes his boy's young. My son was getting too old for him."

"You are one desperate bitch. Lying just so I can let him go and then you can have him back. I'm going back inside."

"Victoria, talk to your son. I know he will tell you what Brody has done. I'm going to the police. Chances are Brody will be in the news. And I can promise you our sons are not the only boys who might come forth."

Melanie takes out a business card of her pocketbook.

"Call me if you want to go to the police with me."

Victoria takes the card.

"You really think this is true?"

"Every part of my being says yes. Please, talk to your son. "

Night has fallen and it is time for rest. Melanie is in her bed sleeping. Her sleep is disturbed by the sound of her phone ringing. She slowly awakes and answers the phone,

"Hello. Who is this, calling me so late?"

"It's me...Victoria."

Melanie quickly sits up and turns on the light near her,

"Hey. What's up?"

"I talked to my son today."

Victoria starts to cry.

"I'm sorry for calling you so late, but I wanted to wait until he fell asleep. He wouldn't stop crying. He told me he knew how happy I was with Brody, so he didn't want to be the reason why the relationship ended. That bastard told my son if he told me what they were doing, he would break up with me and it would be my son's fault. Can you believe him? I just want to go kill him. I need to kill him."

There is a pause. Melanie, please say something

"I'm sorry. I'm…I'm speechless."

"How could you be so speechless? You're the one who told me."

"I know…I'm just…you know… speechless. I just started thinking about something worst then all of this."

"What the hell could be worse than this?"

"Brody broke up with me because my son got too old for him. The question is how many were there before me?"

"Damn, I didn't think of that. Melanie, we have to go to the police."

"I know. Can you meet me there tomorrow?"

"Yes. I want to do it as early as possible."

"Okay."

The very next morning after their sons get to school, Victoria and Melanie get to the police station. Victoria is waiting outside the police station. Melanie pulls up and parks. She gets out of her car and meets up with Victoria. They look at each other both feeling the pain of knowing what happened to their sons. They embrace for a hug and then they enter the station.

CHEN

Cory is sitting in the waiting room of an urgent care. He is reading a magazine when he overhears a conversation between two patients. One of them is reading a newspaper. He leans over to the other patient,

"Can you believe this?"

"What?"

"Did you hear about that Brody guy?"

"I think I did. That's that guy who molested those boys, right?"

"Yeah. Isn't that sad?"

"This world is getting eviler. Is he in prison or did he get bailed out?"

"No, he pleaded guilty. There were fourteen boys who came forth."

"Fourteen? Wow, that's a lot of boys."

"Yeah, according to the news he started when he was eighteen years old. He would look for girls with younger brothers or sons and he would pretend to be interested in the girl. It wouldn't be long before he would find a way to get the boy alone with him."

"That man needs help."

"Yeah, and he's getting it. He has to take group therapy while in prison. The newspaper said he was molested himself."

"You know that molestation is just like a circle."

"How do you mean?"

"You don't know where it begins and when it will end."

"That is sad. All those boys just ruined. I don't understand how every day that goes by, the eviler this world gets."

"Well, the bible did say the world would get eviler because people would more and more stop believing in God and more in themselves. Until the rapture things are only going to get worst."

A nurse is heard,

"Cory Johnson."

Cory takes his case and stands. He follows the nurse to the room. The nurse and Cory enter the room. The nurse prepares the room. Takes Cory temperature and a few other things. She soon finishes and leaves,

"Doctor Song will be in shortly

The nurse leaves the room. Moments later Dr. Song enters,

"Hello, my name is Dr. Song Ching."

"Hi, I'm Cory."

"Hi, Cory. What brings you by today?"

"First, I'd like to thank you for seeing me on such last notice."

"I was told it was an emergency. I usually don't have time for last minute appointments. It must be luck. Why did you need to see me, specifically?"

"It's not luck, it must be fate, or the hand of God."

"What do you mean, Cory?"

"I'm not actually here for medical purposes. Do you have a son named Chen?"

"Yes. Who are you?"

Cory opens his case and takes out his laptop. He opens it and shows it to Song.

"You should read this."

"What is this?"

"It's dialog from your son and I. I met him in a chatroom. Read it."

Song reads the screen.

"That is not my son. He would never speak that way."

110

"Did you read it?"

"Yes, but that doesn't mean anything."

"How else would I have known you worked here? Look, read this."

She reads out loud.

"My mom is a doctor she works at the doctor's office on Fifth Street…my dad is a lawyer. Their jobs keep them away from home so we could meet basically any time. My siblings are barely home either."

Song hangs her head.

"I don't believe this; I can't believe this. Is this a joke? I mean why would he do this? He's a good boy. He gets good grades; he never causes any trouble. Why would he be in a chatroom like this?"

"This doesn't mean he's a bad boy. Let me share something with you. I was molested and after it was all over, I couldn't stop having sex. I searched every where for it. I know it's difficult to believe, but I think your son was molested."

"No. It can't be."

"I don't have time to make you believe. I came here for one reason and one reason only."

"What's that?"

"To make you aware of what your son is doing. I probably wasn't the first person he contacted."

"No. There is just no way."

"Listen, you need to find a way to stay home tomorrow evening. That's when we will be meeting. If you're home, he will have to contact me and break the date. It will be better if he breaks it then me. Then you need to talk to him and figure out why he is doing this. I know this is all shocking and difficult to grasp, but you're going to have to fall apart fast and then quickly put yourself together. Your son needs you. And he needs help."

Cory takes out a business card and hands it to Song,

"Here, take this. She can help Chen."

"What is this?"

"She is a great psychologist. She's the best, trust me, I know. Talk to your son and then get him help."

"Is this real? Is this all real?"

"I know you wish I was lying, but this is real."

"Why didn't you go to the police?"

"Excuse me."

"Why didn't you let the police take care of this? As soon as Chen gave you this information why didn't you go to the police?"

"Because the police don't care about the victims only the suspects. If anything, they would have arrested him."

"Well, thank you for not molesting my son. You could have, but you chose not to. Thank you."

"You're welcome."

Song not able to focus, asks some of the doctors to take her patients. They agree. She asks her boss if she could leave early due to a family crisis. She goes home and reluctantly walks into Chen's bedroom not sure what to do. She stops at the door and sees her son quickly turns off the computer screen. Song asks,

"What was that?"

"What was what?"

"Why did you just turn off the computer?"

"Because I'm done with it."

Song walks to the screen and turns it on. She gasps as she sees gay porn. Chen responds,

"I was just curious. That's all. It doesn't mean anything."

Song turns off the screen,

"I need to talk to you."

"Mom, it's not a big deal. Everyone looks at it."

"It's not about that."

Song takes a brief pause before asking,

"Who is Cory?"

Chen nervously answers

I don't know a Cory."

"He came to my office today. I saw what you wrote to him. Why would you give him my work place? He could have been a murderer for all you know."

"I...I don't know. Did he try to hurt you?"

"No. He's trying to help you."

"What do you mean?"

"How long has this been going on, Chen?"

Chen nervously answers the question,

"It was only last year that it started."

"Are you sexually active with guys of the same age?"

Chen hesitates to answer.

"Not really. We just fool around a bit?"

"Who?"

"It's just me and two other boys from school."

"Why do you guys do this? You are too young to be having sex."

"It just started."

"Who started it?"

"All of us I guess."

"What do you mean?"

"After we left boy scouts, we just…you know. We used to do it all the time on the field trips."

"You mean those trips you went with the boy scouts?"

"Yeah."

"Well, where were the chaperones, the parents? What were they doing?"

"It was one of the chaperones who started it."

Flabbergasted, Song reacts,

"What do you mean?"

"One of the scout leaders would take us into a tent and tell us what to do with each other."

"Are you kidding me?"

"No."

"Which one was it?"

"Mr. Davidson."

"You mean Henry, the one who used to baby-sit you?"

"Yeah."

"Why didn't you tell me!?"

"He told me not to tell anyone. Are you angry with me?"

"No. I'm angry with Henry. You could have told me this."

"Sorry."

"Were you afraid? Did Henry threaten you?"

"He said I can't tell anyone or I would get into trouble. That I might go to jail if I said something."

"So then why did you continue to do it if you knew it was wrong?"

"It's hard to stop once you start."

"He molested you. You realize that, right?"

"I don't know. I guess."

"We have to go to the police, right now, and report him."

"Mom, no. He doesn't do it anymore. Besides don't you have to get back to work?"

"I have a few doctors covering me. And just because he's not molesting you anymore it doesn't mean he stopped molesting. We're going and we're going now. Get your things."

"Mom, I really don't want to."

"Do you want him to continue doing this for the rest of his life? He has to be stopped."

"Can we do it tomorrow?"

"There might be a boy that he chose to molest tomorrow. If we do it today, we can stop him today. Let's go."

Chen reluctantly leaves with his mother.

Song called her husband, Chen's father, and told him to meet them at the police station. They are in an interrogation room. Chen is anxious and filled with fear. Officer Brooks and Officer King enter the room,

"Hi, my name is Officer Brooks and this is my partner Officer King."

"Hi. My name is Song. This is my husband Huang and this our son Chen."

"Is he the one who was molested?"

"Yes."

"Hi, Chen. I'm sorry to hear this. Would you mind telling us who it was and what he did?"

Chen takes a deep breathe.

"His name is Henry Davidson. I first met him when I joined the Boy Scouts. He was one of the leaders. When I was nine, we went on a camping trip. The first time it happened it was me and two of my other friends. He took us into a tent at night and that's when it happened."

Officer King asks,

"Would you mind giving us the names and addresses of your friends, so we can speak with them.

Chen rolls his eyes,

"Do you really need that?"

Officer King replies,

"I know this isn't easy, but we need to confirm what you are saying is true."

Song answers,

"We can give you the information. It's not a problem."

"Thank you."

It's about two days later and Chen is at his locker. Jonathan approaches him,

"Hey, Chen."

"Hey."

"You won't believe what happened."

"What?"

As Jonathan is about to speak, Frederick interrupts them,

"Yo, did the police come to your house?"

Chen uncomfortably answers cautiously,

"No. Why would they?"

"They knocked on my door asking me about Mr. Davidson, about the sex and everything."

Jonathan responds,

"That's what I was just about to say. They came to my house too. That's means they'll be going to you soon."

Chen asks,

"What did you tell them?"

Frederick answers,

"I tried to lie, but they said they had a witness and that he gave them my name. Can you believe that?"

Jonathan responds,

"Really? I wonder who that could be."

Chen pretending to be clueless about the situation,

"Did you tell them anything?"

Jonathan answers,

"Yeah. I told them everything. It just came out. I didn't even mean to."

Chen continues,

"What did your parents think?"

Jonathan answers,

"My dad was angry. I felt so ashamed though. I didn't want him knowing that about me."

Frederick continues,

"My mother cried for hours. It was like as if someone died."

Jonathan asks,

"What are you going to do, Chen?"

"What do you mean?"

"When they come to you?"

"I um...I uh...don't get upset with me, okay?"

Frederick asks,

"What do you mean?"

Jonathan adds,

"Upset about what?"

Chen reluctantly speaks,

"I'm the witness who gave them your names."

Jonathan reacts,

"What the hell is wrong with you?"

Frederick adds,

"Why would you do that?"

"My mom…it's a long story. My mom found out about the molestation. She made me go to the police. I just mentioned you. I don't know why. I don't want to talk about it."

Chen to ashamed to talk about Cory walks away.

JAVIER

Cory is sitting at a booth in a diner. The television can be heard slightly. He reads the closed caption.

"We are outside the Courthouse where Henry Davidson has pleaded guilty to ten counts of Endangerment of a Child. In the past three weeks ten brave boys ranging in the ages from seven to sixteen have come forth confessing they were molested by Mr. Davidson. The judge is in the process of sentencing Mr. Davidson. When we have more information, we will inform you. For now, I'm Suzy Dee with Wolf Five News. Back to you in the studio Jenny."

As Cory watches the television, he overhears a conversation between two customers.

"It seems like every week there is a different guy being arrested for molestation."

"I know. What's going on?"

As Cory takes a sip of his cranberry juice, Lenora walks into the restaurant. She looks around apparently looking for someone. Cory notices her and assumes it's the woman he invited. He raises his hand to get her attention. Lenora notices Cory waving at her. She with anger approaches Cory.

"Are you Cory?"

"Yes, please sit."

"Where is my son?"

"He should be in school."

"Stop playing with me. Where did you put him? If you don't tell me I am going to the police."

"The police can't help. I assure you he's in school."

"Then why did you tell me he was in danger?"

"I said he needed help. I didn't say he was in danger; however, he could be if he keeps it up."

"What the hell are you talking about?"

A waitress approaches the table,

"Can I get you a drink, ma'am?"

"Not now."

"Well, are you guys ready to order?"

Lenora gets frustrated. Cory responds,

"Can you come back in five minutes?"

"Sure."

Corey responds with a thank you and the waitress walks away. Lenora frustrated asks,

"What is going on?"

Cory takes out his laptop from his case. He opens it and shows to Lenora.

"You need to read this."

Lenora reads the screen, her eyes and mouth widened in shock. The waitress returns and sees the expression on Lenora's face and speaks,

"I think I'll give ya'll another five minutes."

Lenora jumps up and rushes home. Cory responds to the waitress,

"No need. I'll take the check."

Lenora awaits her son, Javier. Completely shocked, surprised, and disappointed in herself, she is pacing her living room floor and speaking to herself. She is a true mental mess at the moment. Her front door opens. Javier walks in and Lenora calls for him.

"Javier."

"Hey, ma. You're home early."

"Yes, I am."

Javier walks towards the steps.

"I'll be in my room."

"Javier, I need to speak with you."

"Not now, mom."

"Javier, get over here now!"

"Mom, I have a lot of homework to do."

"Javier Alonzo Fernando, venir aquí ahora mismo."

Javier comes down stairs quickly and approaches his mother.

"Okay, what did I do? Am I in trouble?"

"I received a phone call from a man he told me that you were in trouble and that if I wanted to save you, I should meet him."

"Well, I don't know who that was. I'm okay, momma."

"I went to a diner and met this man and I was completely shocked."

"What are you talking about, ma?"

"The guy's name is Cory."

Javier reacts to the name. Lenora continues,

"Do you know who that is?"

Javier trying to play dumb, asks,

"Who is he?"

"He showed me on his computer the talk the two of you had on the chatroom site. Once you have a taste of me, I promise you, you will come back begging for more. Where the hell did you learn how to talk like that?"

Javier starts crying. Lenora responds,

"My God, he's crying. He is crying. Él está llorando! I thought this was a joke. I thought that man was playing a cruel trick on me, but the fact that you are crying tells me something different. Is this true, Javier, is this true? Did you really make a date with a thrity-five year old man?

Javier doesn't answer.

"Answer me! ¿es cierto"

Javier responds,

"Mom, I'm sorry. Lo Siento."

"Where did you learn this? How did you learn how to do this?"

"I don't know I just did."

"You can't just learn this. Someone had to teach you. I can't understand how a twelve-year-old boy could solicit sex from a thirty-five-year-old man. You're supposed to be playing video games and playing tag with your friends, not having sex with a thirty-five-year-old man. Have you had sex before?"

"Ma, please."

"Answer me, Javier. Have you had sex?"

"I didn't mean to, mom. Te lo prometo."

Javier is sobbing heavily. Lenora embraces him in a hug.

"Shh; quiet. It's okay. Calm down." She continues to embrace him before speaking,

"When was your first time?"

"Do I have to tell? I don't want to?"

"Javier, now listen, I know enough of the truth now. There's no need in keeping anymore secrets. I need you to trust me. Were you molested?"

Javier begins to sob heavily,

"Ma, I don't want to."

"Javier, have you been molested?"

Javier hesitates before he answers

"He still doing it, ma."

"WHO!?"

Cory is watching television in his home. As he flips through the channels he stops on breaking news,

"Are you a former altar boy of St. Christopher's Catholic Church? If you are the police would like to hear from you. Father Clifford Smith of the Catholic Church has been accused of molestation. Because there is only one child at the time accusing him; and because he has pleaded not guilty, the police are looking for possible victims. If you or you know someone who is

or has been molested by the priest please call the police station with any information. Their phone number is 321 555-6987. Any information will be appreciated said Officer Kenneth. I'm Heather Rye reporting from the St. Christopher's Catholic Church. Back to you in the studio."

Two days after the breaking news protestors swarm the church. There are protestors as well as supporters surrounding the church along with media frenzy everywhere. Two police leave the church with Father Clifford in handcuffs. Behind them are two detectives. The police escort Clifford to a police car. The camera crew follows them. A reporter approaches William,

"Can you tell us anything?"

"Hello, my name is William Douglas and I am Father Clifford's lawyer. At this moment there have been five more boys who have come forth claiming that Father Clifford molested them, but at this time Father Clifford maintains his innocence. A trial will begin soon. When I have more information, I will freely share it with you. That is all for now. you may go home now." The media goes wild with more questions. William ignores the inquiries by the press.

A day later Lenora has a meeting with William, but the meeting does not go well. She storms out of the meeting and heads for the exit,

"I don't believe this. This is ridiculous. Esto es increíble. Quiero matarlo."

As she exits a woman notices her and rushes after her.

"Excuse me. Are you Lenora?"

"Yes."

"I saw you on TV. Hi, my name is Catherine. My son was molested by Father Clifford as well."

"Sorry to hear that."

"You seam angry. Is everything okay?"

"I just had a meeting with his lawyer. You won't believe what they asked me."

"What did they say? I have a meeting with them now."

"He wants my son to drop the charges. He said he would pay us three million dollars to drop the charges. With as poor as the church says they are; where the hell are, they going to get that kind of money? Can you believe that?"

"They're probably going to ask me the same thing."

"They'll be surprised when you tell them no, I know they were when I did." Catherine hesitates as she responds,

"Well, we've been having some financial problems."

"What's that supposed to mean?"

"That's a lot of money and we could use it."

"You have to be out of your mind. I can't believe you would allow a predator to walk the streets not to mention run a church, knowing what he did to our sons. Doesn't your son mean anything to you?"

"He does, but we need that money."

"You do realize you are prostituting your son to the church."

"We don't actually know if it's true."

"So, you think your son is lying to you."

"I don't know…I just. This is all too much to bear."

"Yes, it is, but this man deserves to be in prison just like any other abuser. I don't care about his title or reputation. I know my son when he's lying and I can tell he is not lying to me. Come on think about it. Do you actually think your son is lying?" Catherine begins to cry,

"I know he's not, but no one has ever beat the Catholic Church. We cannot win this fight."

"The fight is never over until someone surrenders and I will not surrender."

"I can't fight this battle."

"We have to fight, if not for us for our sons. Don't they deserve it?"

"I just don't know if I can take this journey."

"Catherine, you are not alone. I will fight this battle with you. We can and will win."

Only eight boys came forth to accuse Father Clifford of molestation. However only two families, Lenora and Catherine, have not taken the hush money. Father Clifford has been arraigned, has been sent to prison, with no bail, and has to wait his day in court, where twelve random lives will judge his fate. Lenora was asked by CSB TV to give a statement. Here is her statement,

"I cannot believe the other parents took that money. How low can you be? I will fight until I see justice for my son. Every day we teach our children to tell someone when they have been abused, and when they do; what do we do; we throw three million dollars in their face and tell them to shut up. What hypocrisy is that? The question isn't

any more, how many people have been molested and kept it a secret; the question is now; how many people have confessed and no one did anything about it. My son was brave enough to come forth and I am not about to let money stop him from doing what is right. We are fighting to the bitter end. I hope Father Clifford Smith rots in hell, but until that lucky day, I want to see him go to prison."

Within two weeks of Lenora making her statement for CSB TV, five more families came forth. About five months later, the priest had his day in court. The boys bravely stepped forth and discussed their experiences with the priest. After three long months of this trial, the twelve, went in and came out within two hours with their verdict,

"Foreman, has the jury reached a verdict?"

"Yes, your honor."

"How do you find the verdict?"

"We the jury, find the defendant, Clifford Smith, guilty of seven counts of Child Endangerment."

Father Clifford Smith was the first priest to ever serve prison time for abusing children. He was given ten years per child. Seventy years, he has to spend in prison. After this victory, boys and men every where began to come forth and speak against their abusers.

Even some abusers turned themselves in. You would think Cory would be excited. His work has caused a domino effect of males of all ages receiving justice. But he couldn't seem to stop feeling empty. He couldn't stop feeling guilty.

SEAN

Cory has decided to take a trip back to his therapist. The same doctor he has suggested to the parents of the boys he met online. He is still feeling guilty about his past and needs talking. Cory is in the waiting room. Dr. Karen Zachman walks out of her office and sees Cory,

"Oh, my goodness. I am so glad to see you. Long time no see. How are you doing?

"Okay."

Dr. Karen and Cory walk into her office. They sit.

"So, who are all these people you keep recommending to me?"

"Oh, so they've been calling?"

"Yes. How did you meet these people?"

"Oh, I've been playing police man."

"What do you mean?"

"Well, I've been going to chatrooms. There are many chatrooms out there where boys can hook up with men."

"That's terrible."

"I know. The sad thing is these men are really meeting up with boys and having sex with them."

"How is that possible? Where are the parents of the boys?"

"Usually working. I've been making dates and then meeting up with one of the parents letting them know what was going on. I gave them your business card because you were very helpful to me so I thought maybe you could help out those boys."

"My goodness, Cory. That seems dangerous."

"Yeah, it's worth the sacrifice. Not only do I get help for the boys, but I make the parents aware that there is a chance their son was molested. You know the parents actually contact me once their son's molester is in prison. It's been fulfilling.

"Yeah, but what if the police get involved?"

"It's just a risk I have to take. The police only want to get the molester in prison. They don't care about the victim.

I'm doing this for the victim. And in most cases the suspect is the victim as well.

"Well, I don't know that it is safe and that you should continue to do this. Can't you have the police do it for you?"

"They don't have the same passion as I do. I don't just do it because I want to; I do it because I know I need to do it. No one else is going to care about the prey behind the computer. They only want to see the predator go to prison, but it's so much more than that. If we don't care about the prey; they'll turn into the predator. I'm simply trying to help the victim before they become the suspect.

"You have really thought this through."

"Yes, I have. I actually called because I need to speak with you."

"Oh, why?"

"I'm not feeling well, like I thought I should. I was wondering if I could talk to you. You always knew what to say."

"Not a problem, Cory. My couch is always opened for you. So, tell me what brings you here."

"There is something wrong with me and I am not sure what it is."

"Well, what do you think is wrong?"

"I became a chatroom detective a year ago."

"A year? It's been that long?"

"Yes. I have spoken to twenty-nine mothers and eight fathers. I have helped broken boys get healed and put away over thirty child molesters. I have done more work in a year then the police."

"You sound pleased with yourself."

"That's just the thing. I started this to help people and to make myself feel good about myself, but…I still feel…like there is something missing. I feel like there is more I should be doing and don't know what. I thought helping boys like me would help…you know…remove this guilt."

"What guilt is still there?"

"I'm not sure."

"You have helped over thirty child molesters go to prison."

"Not only that I've helped about fifteen of them get the counseling they needed."

"What about the man who molested you; is he in prison?"

Cory pauses for a moment.

"What does he have to do with anything?"

"You have helped over thirty boys, but you have failed to help yourself."

"You helped me. The counseling I got helped me."

"Your last counseling session was cut short. Remember?"

"I had to leave."

"You never answered my question."

"I don't remember it."

"Did you want me to remind you?"

Cory pauses for a moment. He continues by avoiding the question,

"I'm just trying to get rid of this resentment and bitterness. I thought helping these boys would do that."

"Cory, are you ready to answer my question?"

Cory begins to cry. He ignores the question,

"You know, I had many parents thank me for doing what I did. The appreciation wasn't enough though. It didn't do what I needed it to do."

Karen stays on the subject,

"I'm ready when you're ready."

"I wish someone could have done what I did. I wish someone could have stopped me at younger age. I think I wouldn't have this resentment."

"Do you need a reminder?"

Frustrated, Cory responds,

"No. I don't need a reminder."

"Do you want to answer it?"

Cory pauses before he answers,

"No."

"Well, until you figure that out, that feeling will always be there."

"I am just finding it difficult to forgive."

"Forgiveness is a choice. I think you're trying to feel it. You're not going to feel forgiveness. You just have to choose to do it."

"I'm trying to, but I cannot seem to forget."

"You're not supposed to forget. And unless you get amnesia you won't forget. Forgiveness is not about forgetting; it's about loving someone beyond their falls. God gave us all the power to do it, we just have to choose to use that power. And some times that loving someone beyond their falls is our own selves."

"It's just easier said than done."

"Just about everything is easier said then done, but that doesn't mean you can't do it. It just means you have to work harder to do it. Do you mind if I ask you the question?"

Cory hesitates. He knows he is not ready, but he also knows answering Karen's questions always made his life better,

"Go ahead."

"Have you forgiven yourself yet?"

Pretending he doesn't understand the question, Cory responds,

"Why would I need to forgive myself?"

"Your cousin."

Cory cries. He pauses to think.

"I tried, but I can't seem to do it. I feel like I messed him up."

"Well, that's why you can't forgive, because you haven't forgiven yourself. Love, forgiveness, peace, and joy all start with you. You can't give it to anyone until you have given it to yourself."

"So, once I choose to forgive myself, you think I'll be able to forgive my abuser."

"Yes. It's difficult, but yes."

"Thank you, Dr. Zachman. I knew I could count on you. I'm sorry for abruptly running out in our last session, but I wasn't ready. And I am sorry for not contacting you for so long."

"I know. I'm just glad you're ready now. Take it one day at a time."

"I will. Thank you."

"You're welcome."

After meeting with his therapist, Cory takes the plunge and visits his cousin, Sean. Sean unaware of his visit lights up when he sees Corey,

"Hey, cuz, what are you doing here?"

"Hey, Sean. I came to see you."

"Well, come on in."

Cory walks in the room. Sean embraces Cory with a hug. Cory with much guilt receives the hug. Cory speaks,

"What a surprise. It's been so long."

"Yeah, I know. I just wanted to talk to you."

"Oh sure. Is everything okay?"

"Yeah. You mind if I sit?"

"Not at all."

Cory sits on the couch, Sean joins him. Concerned, Sean asks,

"So, what's up?"

"I just came to…you know…apologize."

"Apologize? For what?"

"You know…for what I did to…you know…when we were children."

"Oh. Ah, man that's water under the bridge. No need in bringing that up."

"No, I had to formally apologize to you. I needed you to know that I am sorry and that I fully regret doing that to you. I didn't know whether or not you forgave me. I know I haven't been able to forgive myself just yet. My therapist told me I needed to forgive myself in order to forgive…anyway I just wanted to say I'm sorry."

"It's okay, man, I forgave you already."

Cory looks speechless.

"So, that's it? You're okay? You're not upset?"

"No. Why would I be upset?"

"Because I molested you, Sean. I'm your cousin. You were supposed to trust me and I abused you. You're supposed to be angry and bitter."

"No, I forgave you. All that is over. I know you meant no harm. I didn't understand it then, but I am old enough to understand it now."

"But you should still be a little angry. I took your innocence away from you, I stole your virginity. You should be upset with me for what I've done to you."

"I was. There was a time when I was, but I've learned forgiveness. It is not an easy thing to do, but with much counseling I was able to forgive myself and then you."

"But I never apologized until now. How could you forgive me?"

"Forgiveness is a choice. Whether you apologize or not I chose to forgive you."

"I don't understand that. Don't you want to hit me; don't you want to see me in prison? Why didn't you call the police on me? Didn't you think that I could still be out there doing what I did to you?"

"I never thought of that. Why are you so angry? I told you I forgave you."

"Because you should feel pain. You should feel like hurting me, you should feel violated, you should feel like getting revenge. Why don't you have those feelings?"

"I once did, but it slowly went away as I forgave you."

Cory stands,

"I want you to hit me."

"What?"

Hit me; hurt me. Punch me. Make me feel the pain I gave you."

"The pain you gave me I cannot give to you with a hit."

Those words were a punch in the heart. Cory sits and responds,

"So, you're angry about that, aren't you? That makes you angry, doesn't it?"

Cory stands,

"It won't be the same, but you will feel better, just do it. Hit me, please."

"Cory, what is wrong with you?"

Cory is crying

"There is nothing wrong with me. I'm just trying to figure out how to forgive him when this pain won't go away. I want to hurt him; I want to hurt him really badly and I don't understand why you don't feel the same. Make me pay for what I did to you. Hit me!"

Sean embraces Cory and hugs him. Cory is sobbing. Sean asks,

"You never cried, did you?"

"No."

"You need to cry, Cory. That's the first step of forgiveness."

Cory sobs heavily. He embraces Sean as if he's afraid Sean will let go. Sean holds him tighter assuring him he won't leave him. Sean allows Cory to cry as long as needed.

CORY

Esther walks to her mailbox and empties it. With surprise she has received a letter from her son, Cory. Cory hasn't spoken to his mother in ten years. He ignored her calls and letters. He finally had the courage, the boys he helped, had. Esther, surprised and happy to finally hear from him, rushes inside her house and opens the letter immediately. She rips it open like a child opening a present on Christmas day. She smiles as she see's the letter. Her heart is happy, but that is because she is unaware of what the letter says. She smiles and begins to read,

"Dear mom, first, please forgive me for ignoring you for the past ten years. There is no excuse for my behavior and lack of honoring you. I do love you and miss you, but I couldn't seem to see you and that is not your fault. I am sorry for moving out without letting you know. For just leaving abruptly. It was wrong and I should have not done it, but I was afraid and didn't know what else to do. As you know, when I was younger, I would always ask you if I could move in with dad, instead of living with you and Timothy. I never meant to break your heart by asking you that. I did not love dad more than you, I just wanted to be free from Timothy. I don't know how to say this without hurting you, but when you weren't home, Timothy would *molest me. I always wanted to tell you before you left, as well as when you came back home, but the words never seemed to leave my lips. I know how much you loved Timothy, so I felt bad letting you know what he was doing to me. At your wedding, my behavior was inexcusable, but I was young and wasn't sure how to deal with the fact that my abuser would be living with me. The thing is Timothy never stopped molesting me until I moved out, ten years ago. By the time I was twenty I was old enough to stop it, but I've gotten so used to it, I chose not to continue. I hated when you went to work, I hated what Timothy was doing to me, and I hated myself for not saying anything. Thanks to therapy, I now realize that is why it took me so long to forgive him. Just so you know I repeated what Timothy did to me with Sean. Every time Aunt Bernice and Sean came over, just as long as ya'll went shopping, me and him would, well, you know. I have recently spoken to Sean and apologized. He forgave me for what I did to him before I was even able to forgive myself. I don't know if Timothy is still doing those things or if he got help, but I needed you to know what he did to me and I need you to tell him that I forgive him. I cannot go to the police because it is way past the statues of limitations. When you are ready you can come visit me. Along with this letter is my business card. On the back is my home address. My phone number is on it too so you can call me. Sorry for staying away for so long, but I didn't know how to deal with Timothy. I know this is not your fault, but I just couldn't face him. Please forgive me for running away from you and not staying in contact. I meant no harm; I was just hurt. I love you mom."*

Love,

Corey Barker

Esther crumbles the letter and lets out a screeching yell. Timothy rushes to her and asks,

"What's wrong with you?"

She screams and then lunges at Timothy. She punches and slaps and kicks him, while yelling,

"You're a pervert. A disgusting pervert. How could you do that to my baby?"

"What are you talking about? Stop, woman!"

He grabs her arms and looks her in the eyes,

"What is wrong with you, Esther?"

She gets a hold of herself. She throws the letter at him and speaks,

"Read the letter. I've got to go."

Esther grabs her pocketbook and leaves the house. Timothy picks up the letter and reads it. With much shock and shame, he sits down in a chair and sobs. After about an hour he begins to prepare to discuss the matter with Esther. However, his plans fail, when he hears sirens arriving to his home. With confusion he stands and goes towards the door. Of course, as nosey as they are, the neighbors come out of their homes to see what the sirens are about. The police knock on the door and Timothy answers it with tears still rolling from his eyes. They speak with Timothy for a bit and then inform him of Esther turning him in. He simply nods and cooperates with the police. They arrest him and take him to the station.

Although it was too late for Cory to receive justice, Esther was aware of the many times Timothy babysat the neighbor's children. Once Timothy made the news, the neighbors began to ask their children, and some of the boys bravely came forward. Timothy plead guilty and was sentence to thirty-five years in prison.

Esther took some time to visit Cory. They had a crying session and an apology session afterwards. Their relationship has been mended and Cory has finally begun to heal from his past.

Now that he is fulfilled, he has decided to take Dr. Karen's advice and involved the police in his chatroom detecting. Him and the police have now helped over hundred different boys seek the help they need and have helped stopped boys from meeting up with men for sex.

NOAH

Cory is sitting in his car. He opens the door and gets out with his case. He walks to the door and rings the door bell. A man comes to the door,

"May I help you?"

"Are you Wade?"

Concerned, Wade asks,

"Yes, who are you?"

"Do you have a son named, Noah?"

"Yes. Please tell me who you are?"

"I'm going to need you to step outside. I need to talk to you about your son. It's urgent."

"What is going on?"

Cory takes his case and opens it. He takes out the laptop and hands it to Wade.

"Open it and read it."

"Why?"

"Please, just do it."

Wade reads it and then looks at Cory in shock.

"That's my information?"

"Who is this?"

"bigblack35 is me, theflood69 is your son. He contacted me for sex. I simply came here to let you know so you can stop him before it gets out of hand."

This is the end of this book, but, unfortunately not the end of the story. It is reported that girls are molested more than boys, but I disagree. Girls speak up more than boys do. I believe boys are abused more, but are too fearful to admit it. I hope this book brings hope and bravery to males to not only speak up against their abusers, but to turn themselves in, if they are an abuser.

RAINN (Rape, Abuse & Incest National Network)
800-656-HOPE (4673)
rainn.org

National Domestic Abuse Hotline
1-800-799-SAFE

Child Abuse Hotline
1-800-4-A-CHILD

inhope.org

childhelp.org/hotline

Rohkea Campana

Abioye Lekan Zuberi saves America from injustice, inequality, white privilege and discrimination, by becoming the king of America. How does he do it? Check out "Saving America."

lucylleftiepublishing.weebly.com